THIS **Elephant & Piggie** BOOK
BELONGS TO:

To Lee and Diane

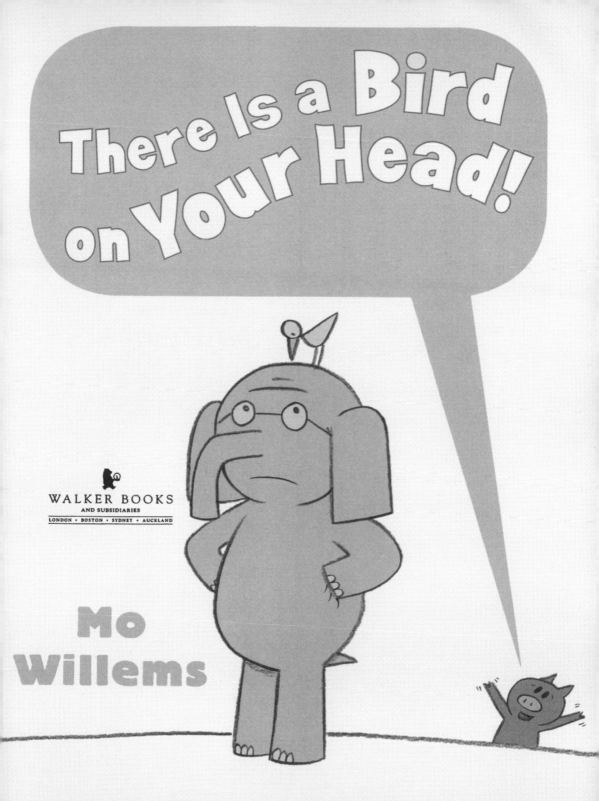

There Is a Bird on Your Head!

Mo Willems

WALKER BOOKS
AND SUBSIDIARIES
LONDON · BOSTON · SYDNEY · AUCKLAND

An **Elephant & Piggie** Book

6

There is a bird
on my head?

aggghhh!!!

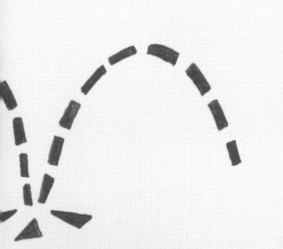

Is there a
bird on my
head now?

13

Now there are two birds on your head.

What are two birds doing on my head?

They are
in love!

The birds on my head are in love?

They are love birds!

How do you know they are love birds?

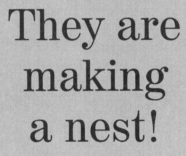

They are
making
a nest!

22

Two birds are
making a nest
on my head?

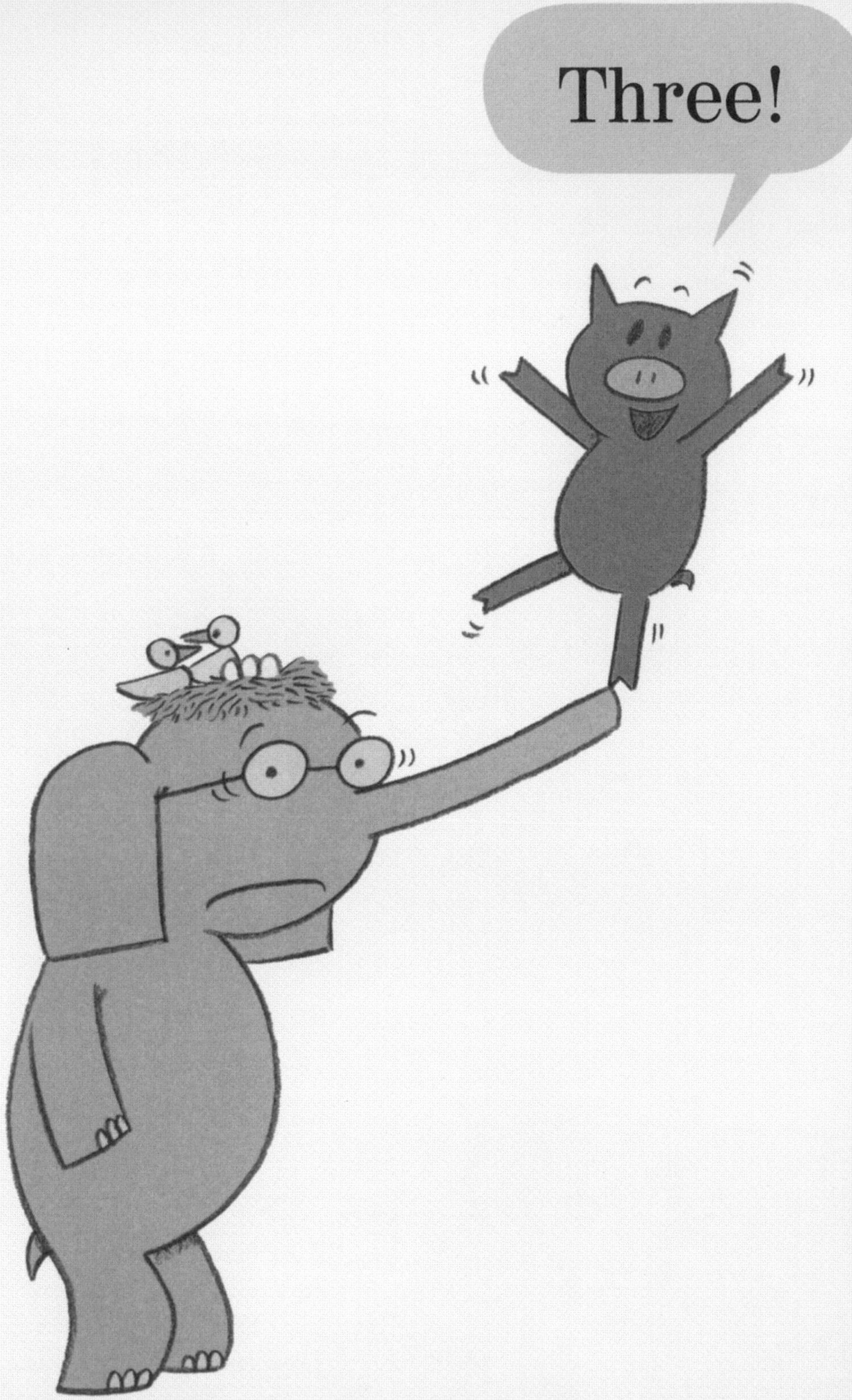
Three!

You have three eggs
on your head.

34

The eggs are gone?

The eggs are hatching!

HATCHING?

41

Now I have three
baby chicks on
my head!

And two birds
and a nest!

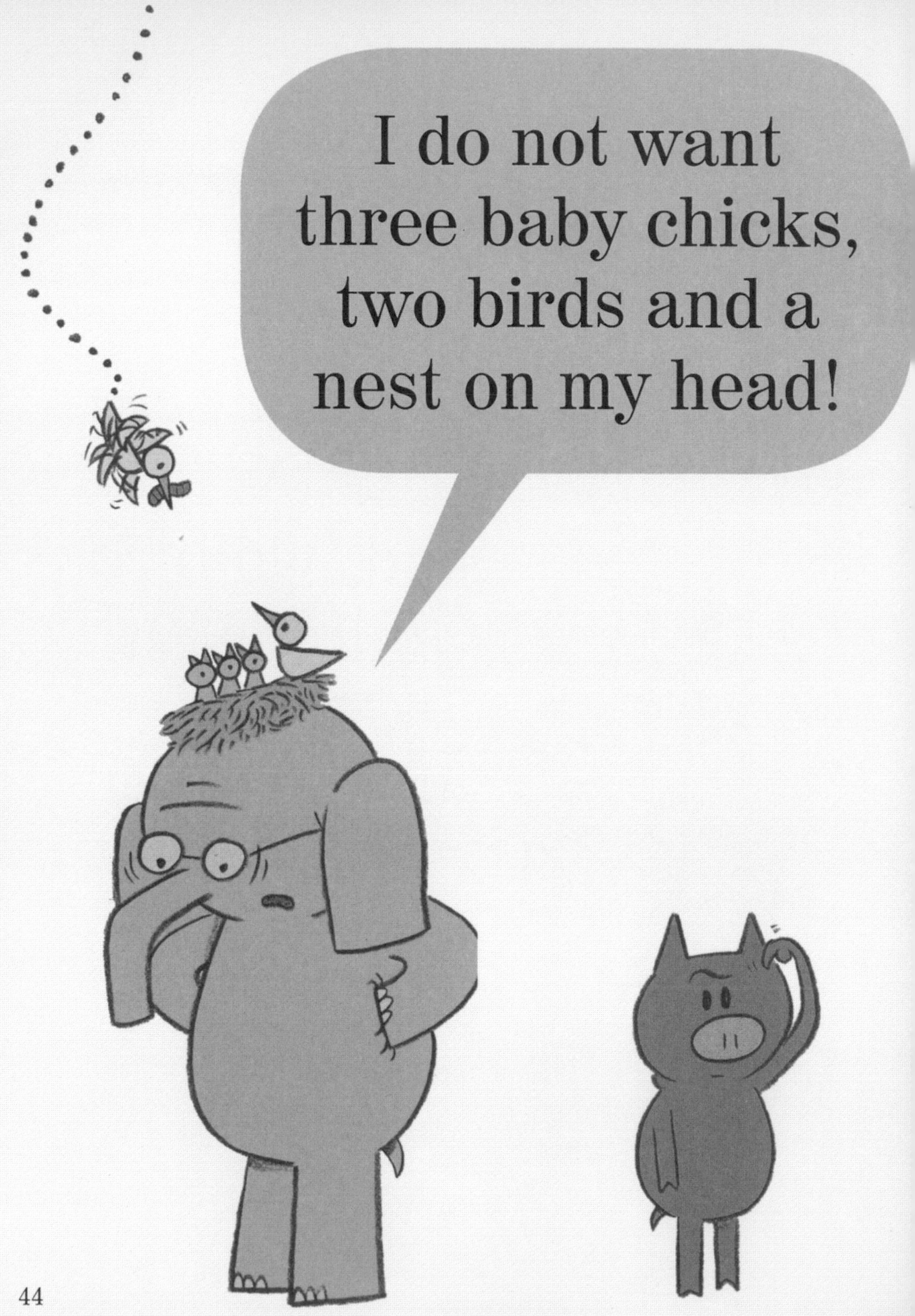
I do not want three baby chicks, two birds and a nest on my head!

Where do you want them?

46

Why not ask them to go somewhere else?

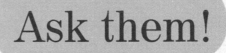

53